Lalo Wants a  Real Name

written by
Julia Mercedes Castilla

illustrated by
Stephanie Harlow

"Lalo, it's time to come in. It's getting late."

Abuela yelled from the house.

Lalo did not answer.

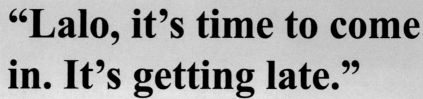

"Who's Lalo?"
asked a red-haired boy who was
playing with a stick by the sidewalk.

"I don't know,"
Lalo answered while making faces at the little
girl he was playing with in the front yard.

Lalo was staying at his grandparents' house in Houston while his parents were on a trip. He loved to visit his grandparents in the big city since he lived in a small town in West Texas. They took him to the ice cream store, to the park, and sometimes Lalo went with his grandfather, Papo, to the zoo. Lalo loved to pet the animals. This visit was special to him. His *abuelos* were taking him to the big circus tomorrow.

"Lalo?" yelled *Abuela* again. **"I don't want to have to drag you in here. Papo is waiting."**

She stood at the front door.

"She's calling you Lalo," the little girl said.

"Yeah, your grandmother doesn't call you Bobby," the red haired boy said, still poking the ground with the stick.

"I said my name is Bobby." Lalo walked toward the house.
The children followed him.

The red haired boy stood in front of *Abuela*.

"He said his name is Bobby."

"He said that? Well... maybe he turned himself into Bobby. I wonder where Lalo is?

"I don't want to play with you."
Lalo stuck out his toungue at the children and went inside.

"Why did you tell them your name is Bobby?"
Abuela asked.

"No one is called Lalo.
I want to have a real name,
like Bobby or Jimmy."

"Last week you told your kindergarten teacher your name was Matthew. What has gotten into you my boy?"

"Lalo is a silly name. Now my name is Bobby Brown."

"It's about time you came in. I'm starving,"
Papo said, his big belly laughing along with him as he walked to the table to join the small-rounded figure of Abuela.

Lalo loved to lean against his grandmother's soft stomach while she told him stories of the old country-- "*mi país*", as she called her birthplace.

Lalo's mind was on the most important event in his life.

THE CIRCUS! He could hardly wait until tomorrow to see the elephants, the tigers and the clowns. He had never been to a big circus. His mother took him once to see the clowns at the mall, but that was not a real circus.

"No cookies until you eat your dinner," Papo said as Lalo picked one from a plate.

"His name is Bobby Brown. He doesn't like a strange name like Lalo." said *Abuela*.

"Bobby Brown?" Papo asked. "Then you're not related to us, right? Our last name isn't Brown, but Ramos."

"Where did Lalo go? We love him and miss him,"
Abuela looked serious.

"Bobby, sit down and eat your dinner."

Lalo did not say anything. He did not like his grandmother calling him Bobby. He would not have liked his mother calling him Bobby either. What did Papo mean when he said he was not related to them? They were his *abuelos*.

"We're going to the circus tomorrow.
                              You promised."

"Yes, but we promised to take Lalo Ramos, not Bobby Brown. Now go get ready for bed," *Abuela* ordered.

Lalo did not sleep well. He dreamed he was living in a big house with strange parents he did not like, and children sticking out their tongues at him.

He awoke mumbling "Lalo, Lalo."
The familiar sound of his name made him feel good.

"Do you want cereal for breakfast?" asked Papo.

Abuela was taking the cereal box out of the pantry.
"I don't know if Bobby Brown likes cereal?"

"I like cereal with lots of milk. Abuela, I want you to call me Lalo. I don't care if I don't go to the circus. I'd like you to be my grandparents again."

"Of course we are, and we want to go to the circus with you," Papo said.

"My name is Lalo. I'm not Bobby Brown. I don't want you to say that I am not related to you."

Lalo looked down so his grandparents would not see the tears in his eyes.

"We are your grandparents. We love our grandson, Lalo, very much. Come here child."

Papo sat him on his big belly and tickled him.

"Let's have breakfast."

"**Are we going to the circus after breakfast?**"
Lalo dared ask.

"**Yes, we are in a little while,**" *Abuela* said, pouring milk in Lalo's cereal bowl.

"My name is Lalo!
My name is Lalo!"

Lalo stood in front of his grandparents.

"Someone is at the door," *Abuela* said at the sound of the doorbell.

Lalo ran over to open it.

"Hi," he said to the little girl he had played with the day before

"Do you want to go out and play?"
she asked.

**"Okay, but only for a while. Later my
grandparents are taking me to the circus."**

"The circus? I want to go to the circus too."
The little girl jumped from place to place.

"Let's go play, Bobby. I like the name Lalo better, like your grandmother calls you.
I like to play with Lalo."

Lalo Ramos was not a silly name after all.
It was a good name and it was his.

"Sounds good," he said to himself.
Lalo felt warm all over and decided to
continue to be called Lalo Ramos.

First English Edition

ISBN-13: 978-1-62395-709-4

eISBN: 978-1-62395-634-9

Published in the United States by Xist Publishing

www.xistpublishing.com

PO Box 61593 Irvine, CA 92602

xist Publishing

Made in the USA
Monee, IL
24 September 2022

14541249R00021